HOT HiPPO

HODDER CHILDREN'S BOOKS

First published in Great Britain in 1986 by Hodder Children's Books
This edition published in 2016 by Hodder and Stoughton

29

A CIP catalogue record for this book
is available from the British Library.

ISBN 978 0 340 41391 3

Printed in China

The paper and board used in this book
are from wood from responsible sources.

Hodder Children's Books
An imprint of
Hachette Children's Group
Part of Hodder and Stoughton
Carmelite House
50 Victoria Embankment
London EC4Y 0DZ

An Hachette UK Company
www.hachette.co.uk

www.hachettechildrens.co.uk

HOT HIPPO

BY
Mwenye Hadithi

iLLUSTRATED BY
ADRienne Kennaway

Hodder
Children's
Books

Hippo was
hot.

He sat on the river bank and gazed at the little fishes swimming in the water.

If only I could live in
the water, he thought,
how wonderful life would be.

So he walked and he ran and he strolled
and he hopped and he lumbered along until
he came to the mountain where Ngai lived.

Ngai was
the god of Everything
and Everywhere.

Ngai told the animals to live on the land and the fishes to live in the sea.

Ngai told the birds to fly in the air and
the ants to live under the ground.

Ngai had told Hippo he was to live
on the land and eat grass.

"Please, O great Ngai, god of Everything and
Everywhere, I would so much like to live in the
rivers and streams," begged Hippo hopefully.

"I would still eat grass."

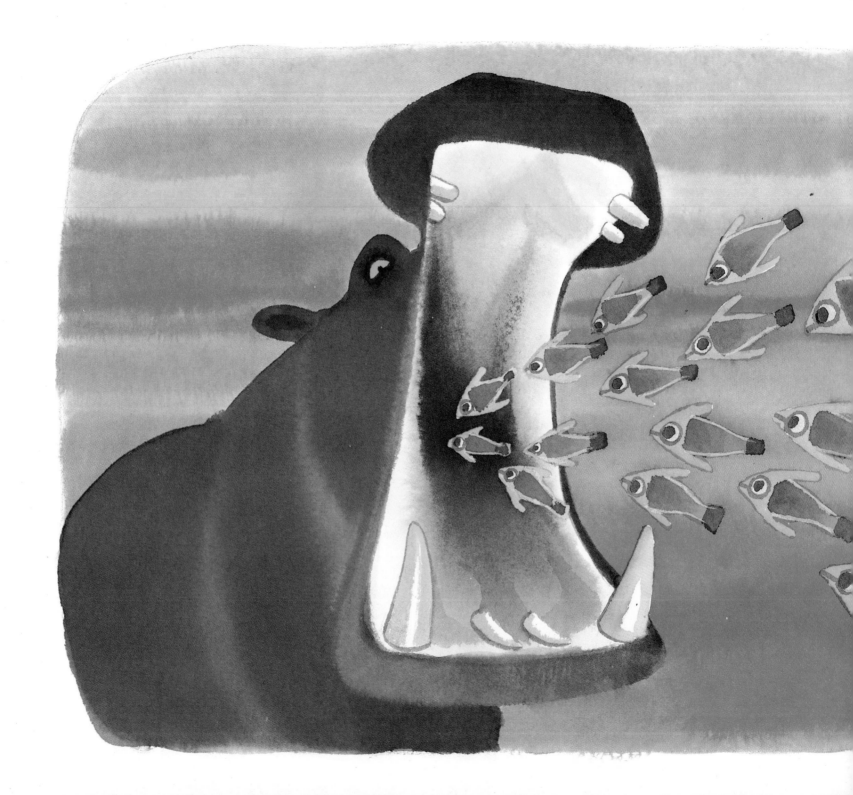

"Aha!"

thundered the voice of Ngai.
"So you say. But one day you might, just
might, eat a fish to see if it tasted good.
And then you would
EAT ALL MY LITTLE FISHES!"

"Oh no, I promise I wouldn't," said Hippo.

"Aha!"

thundered the voice of Ngai.
"So you say! But how can I be sure of that?
I LOVE MY LITTLE FISHES!"

"I would show you," promised Hippo.
"I will let you look in my mouth
whenever you like, to see that I am
not eating your little fishes."

"And I will stir up the water with my tail so you can see I have not hidden the bones."

"Aha!"

thundered the voice of Ngai.
"Then you may live in the water but..."

Hippo waited...

"...but you must come out of the water at night and eat grass, so that even in the dark I can tell you are not eating my little fishes. Agreed?"

"Agreed!" sang Hippo happily.

And he ran all the way home until
he got to the river, where he
jumped in with a mighty

SPLASH!

And he sank like a stone,
because he couldn't swim.

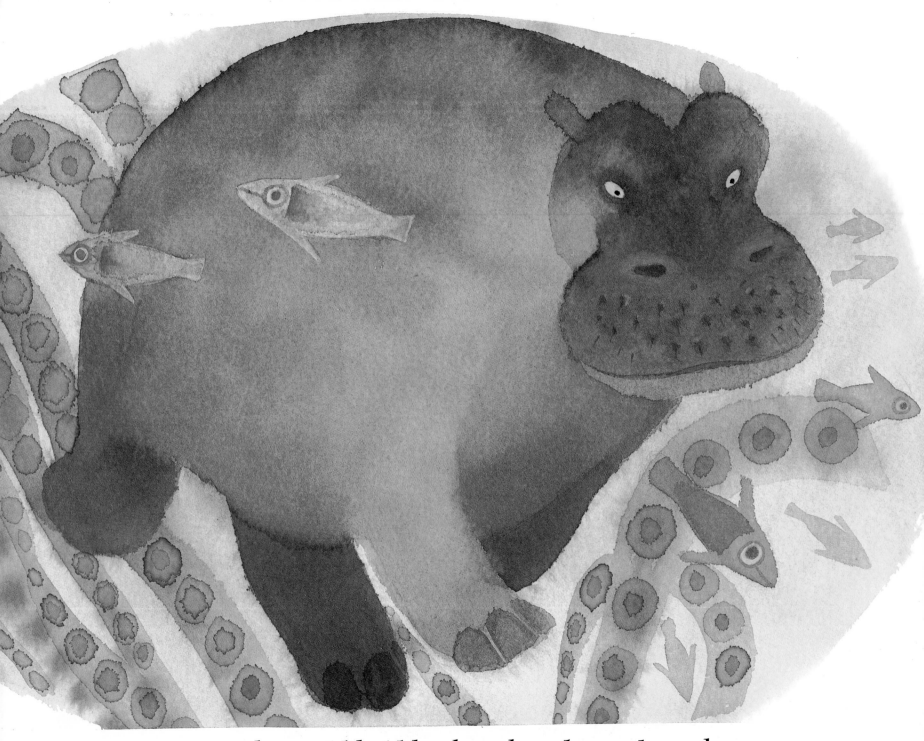

But he could hold his breath and run along the
bottom which he does to this very day.

And he stirs up the bottom by wagging his little tail,
so that Ngai can see he has not hidden any fish-bones.

And now and then he floats to the top and opens his huge mouth ever so wide and says: "Look, Ngai! No fishes!"